BLOOD AND BLOODY PROFANITY

A WILKINSON'S DETECTIVE AGENCY SHORT STORY

ALEXANDRIA BLAELOCK

Also by Alexandria Blaelock

SHORT STORY COLLECTIONS
The Haunting of Hayward Hall
Lovelorn, Lovestruck and Love at First Sight
Common or Garden Variety Heroes
Case Files of the Wilkinson Detective Agency
Unavoidable Fates
Christmas Travesties
Five Faces of Felicia Clarke

FICTION
That Love Nonsense
Taipan vs Brown

MS BLAELOCK'S BOOKS
Stress Free Dinner Parties
Signature Wardrobe Planning
Holistic Personal Finance
Minimally Viable Housekeeping
Planning a Life Worth Living

A SELECTION OF AVAILABLE SHORT STORIES
Alma'that thas Grace
Fate in Your Hands
Kiss of Death
Lady of the Looking Glass
Life in the Security Directorate
Morning Star, Evening Star, Superstar
Payton's Run
Secret Singer
Shining Star
Ship in a Bottle
Simone Says Hands in the Air
The Day the Schedule Broke

BLOOD AND BLOODY PROFANITY

A WILKSINSON'S DETECTIVE AGENCY SHORT STORY

ALEXANDRIA BLAELOCK

BlueMere Books
MELBOURNE, AUSTRALIA

For permission requests, please contact enquiries@bluemerebooks.com.

Ordering Information:
Discounts are available on quantity purchases. For details, contact orders@bluemerebooks.com.

Blood and Bloody Profanity/Alexandria Blaelock
paperback ISBN: 978-1-922744-65-4
digital ISBN: 978-1-922744-66-1

Book Layout © BookDesignTemplates.com
Cover Art © Benoit Daoust/Depositphotos

BLOOD AND BLOODY PROFANITY

Phoebe Swan stood, concealed by a grove of trees, looking down over the grave.

The exhumation represented the worse possible outcome, of her worst possible case.

The morning sun shone brightly, the air quiet and still, without the hint of a breeze.

Just as it had been the day of almost sixteen-year-old Lette Walker's funeral.

Only without the scene of pink-clad mourners bellowing like cows at milking time.

Sweat trickled down her sides, making a mockery of her deodorant manufacturer's claim of 72 hours of dryness.

She *could* have worn something cooler and lighter than her black crepe pants suit, but black was how she felt as well as how she was.

Any other colour would have felt like a mockery.

She could see silhouettes against the brightly lit sides of the tent they worked within. Police clustered on one side, watching the gravediggers work.

Where they'd once lowered Lette out in the open, now they lifted her in private.

If only time reversed itself at the same moment.

She'd been the one who was supposed to find the kidnappers, catch them, and bloody well bang them up.

Before they killed the girl, and before they fled with the money.

And even though Inspector Mason had revealed the information to the kidnappers, she'd taken responsibility. She'd quit, while he'd stayed in the force, "earning" a promotion.

For the sake of future victims, she hoped he was incompetent and not corrupt. But regardless of how or why he did what he did, neither was a good outcome.

She'd chosen to suffer, and suffer she had throughout the intervening decade.

Moped for a while, then got her Private Security licence and joined the Wilkinson National Detective Agency. Established 1889.

Joining a long, and proud history that had come a long way since those early days of divorces, perjury, and trespass.

Because despite everything, she was still a good investigator. And still felt compelled to right the wrongs.

It was her habit to talk to Lette when she ran into an issue she needed to work through.

Because no one listens better than the dead.

And often a quiet moment with Lette did help clear the brain and get the neurons firing.

But if Lette wasn't there...

She watched the exhumation a little longer, wondering why, and who, and how it had come about.

And then she sighed and turned away, almost running straight into Lette's mother; Grace Walker, the last person she wanted to see.

Who'd lost half her body weight, and seemingly three-quarters of her wits in the decade since Phoebe had last seen her; when Lette had been laid to rest.

Phoebe nodded and attempted to walk past her, but Mrs Walker, wild grey hair standing on end, caught her sleeve in a surprisingly strong grip, effectively preventing her escape.

Phoebe turned her head to look at Mrs Walker, who said, "you can see we're bringing her out."

Not trusting her voice, she nodded.

"We want to know what happened."

Phoebe nodded again and attempted to walk away, but the older woman held her jacket fast.

"We don't want no uppity bloke telling us what's what this time. We want you.

Surely that had to be an exaggeration, she shook her head.

Mrs Walker shook the arm of Phoebe's jacket, and her arm with it.

"You. You always told us straight. You were always fair and reasonable until that Inspector turned up."

Phoebe cleared her throat, "I'm not with the Police anymore. I'm a Wilkinson investigator now."

"That's right. Private now."

"You can't just come to me; you'll have to go through the office. And I'm on another case anyway."

"We want *you*."

Phoebe sighed; she just wasn't getting through to the woman.

"Come with me, we'll sort something out."

《《 • 》》

Phoebe sat in a white interrogation room; no windows, no clocks, and grey linoleum on the floor. There was nothing, aside from the scuff marks on the walls to look at.

The room was furnished with a battered table, two chairs on one side, and a hard chair with one slightly bent leg on the other.

She was fairly sure it was an attempt to undermine her confidence.

The wonky chair was an old interrogation technique; most people couldn't sit still, or get comfortable, but would rock backwards and forwards as they tried to maintain their balance.

She, however, had learned a lot about bullying and intimidation during her time with Wilkinson's. She sat up; spine straight, feet firmly on the floor, leaning slightly back. She closed her eyes, folded her hands in her lap and waited.

Perfectly still.

Fortunately, she had plenty to think about.

Starting with how quickly Grace Walker had convinced her boss Sharon to allocate the case to her.

And what she'd said that had convinced Sharon to take all Phoebe's other cases away so she'd have no choice but to devote all her time and energy to Lette's case.

Not to mention, that Sharon had given her full access to all the resources and services Wilkinson's offered.

And biggest of all, what exactly Grace Walker hoped to achieve.

So, giving it the most charitable interpretation of events.

1. Lette had been kidnapped.

2. The kidnappers had demanded a ransom of $100,000.

3. The Walkers had taken out a loan.

4. Mason made the drop and walked away - in full view of at least six undercover Police Officers.

5. No one saw the moment when the money was taken.

6. The money was never recovered.

7. The kidnappers claimed not to have received the payoff.

8. A few days later, after a series of increasingly angry phone conversations, Lette's badly beaten body had been dumped.

9. The body was rushed through forensics, then released, and out the door to the funeral home.

10. Buried, in retrospect, with what seemed like indecent haste.

It was a harsh lesson for the Walkers - who had to deal with bankruptcy while they grieved.

But as far as anyone else was concerned, at least the body had been recovered, and they weren't left wondering.

So, at this point, she had to go back to basics.

And given the Walkers were funding the exhumation and subsequent forensic pathology...

She started listing the factors.

1. Was the body was in fact, Lette?
2. If not, who was it?
3. Why was she substituted for Lette?
4. How had the substitute died?
5. Where the hell was Lette?

Someone high up in Wilkinson's had leaned on someone high up in the Police, who had given her permission to view the file and her case notes to refresh her memory.

The door jerked open, and judging by the heavy tread, a large, male Police Officer strode in.

"Napping on the job eh Swan?" Mason asked.

She waited for a moment before opening her eyes, and looked up at him. Framing himself in the door.

Time had not been kind to his face, even if it had his shoulder. He'd let himself go; too many political dinners and not enough time in the gym.

She raised an eyebrow, "are you slumming it down here Superintendent Mason? Don't you have any big cases upstairs that need your attention more?"

He crossed the floor in two steps, and leaned one hip against the table, slapping the file against the other, "as the officer in charge of this investigation, I thought it prudent to at least see what you have."

"Wilkinson's has just allocated the case to me," she said, showing him her license card, but didn't let him remove it from her fingers, "I don't have anything to share yet."

He grunted, "well, I hope you don't mind, but I'll be watching you to ensure you don't remove anything from the file."

Phoebe smiled, a straight, thin smile - she'd been expecting that, "I'm not sure why you refused to prepare an evidence brief for the Walker's lawyers. That seems fishy to me."

He stood, and flung the file on the desk, "you have one hour."

Still smiling, she nodded, and pulled the wonky chair closer to the table.

He paced the length of one side of the room as she took out her daybook and opened the file at the beginning.

He paced along the second wall as she started to read, and jotted down her first note.

He paced out the third wall as she took her first photo of an evidence report.

He paced out the fourth wall, and she watched him from under the cover of her lowered eyelids.

So this was how he wanted to play it.

She was a little surer now that he had something to do with the disappearance of the money. Though she still had no proof.

She ignored him as he continued pacing in circles, clockwise then anticlockwise, occasionally knocking her chair, as she continued to study the file for the rest of the hour.

An alarm went off somewhere on his person, his watch or his phone, and he swooped on the file, knocking her phone to the floor.

She left it where it was, "I'll take my notebook and fountain pen if you please."

He made a show of reading over her notes, not that it mattered as she'd written it in her version of shorthand - almost indecipherable to herself let alone others.

She caught her fountain pen as he dropped it, hoping he hadn't bent the nib. There was next to nowhere left in Melbourne where she could fix it.

She swapped the lid from the post to the nib, collected her phone from the floor, and held out her hand for the book.

He dropped it on the desk and left the room.

Mason was as arrogant as ever.

But the tricks that had worked on her a decade ago, were useless now. She wasn't a probationary detective anymore. And he was nowhere near as impressive physically or intellectually.

She added a question to her list:

6. What the hell did Mason have to hide?

《《 • 》》

With the resources of Wilkinson's at her back, the next step was to visit the Victorian Institute of Forensic Medicine to see what they'd found.

She was escorted to a neat, clean meeting room by a young, and seemingly efficient man, "Dr Daniels is just finishing up her report and will be with you shortly. Can I get you something to drink?"

Phoebe declined, but he brought a jug of cold water and a couple of glasses on a tray anyway. It made her want coffee, but she didn't tell him she'd changed her mind.

He clearly had more important things to do.

At least this room had chairs with four even legs and an outside view over the Coroner's Court.

It could be considered comfortable, though its purpose wasn't to make hardened criminals confess.

She took out her daybook and started going through her notes.

"Hello," a tall, blonde woman said as she walked through the door and closed it behind her. "I'm Dr Jane Daniels, how are you?"

"Phoebe Swan, Wilkinson's Investigator," she said standing up to shake the woman's hand.

Jane laid a manilla folder on the table in front of Phoebe, "I don't believe this body is that of Lette Walker."

Phoebe frowned at the file without opening it, "what makes you say that?"

Jane sat at the table and poured two glasses of water, "This girl was riddled with cancer, and was receiving treatment for several months before she died, whereas Lette was fit and well.

"My guess is this body was taken from a funeral home sometime between the funeral and the inhumation."

Phoebe scratched her forehead with the tip of her capped fountain pen, "if she's not Lette do you know who she is?"

"Not yet, the body's been turned over to the Human Identification team."

"Is that not the kind of thing that should have been discovered in the first autopsy?"

"I would have thought so."

Phoebe listed out the sequence on her fingers, "so, someone, possibly the kidnappers, took a corpse from the mortuary.

"Smashed the girl's face in, hoping her identity wouldn't be discovered.

"Dressed her in Lette's clothes.

"The Pathologist rushed the autopsy.

"And the Police closed the investigation without actually investigating it."

Jane folded her hands on the desk, "I really wouldn't like to comment."

"I assume you're referring the body back to the Police?"

"We'll definitely have to at some point - we now have a missing person *and* an unidentified body.

"But as Wilkinson's commissioned the exhumation on behalf of the Walkers, we'll have to conclude your work first."

"I see, so for the moment, your team and I are the only ones who know about this?"

Jane nodded.

"Then you'll keep me up to date with the identity of the girl?"

"Of course. We've got some viable DNA, and we're running it through the databases we have access to, but the death was a decade ago, so I don't expect much from that avenue. I'll get someone to comb the registry of deaths to see if we can find a match."

"Thanks, that will definitely help. Anything else?"

"I've asked the team to do a facial reconstruction," Jane smiled, "If nothing else, given the girls are about the same age, it's possible the Walker's might know, and recognise her."

"I didn't see any reference to Lette's DNA analysis in the case file of the original investigation, but I know took samples from Lette's hairbrush at the time."

"I'll see if there's any record of it here, but it might be quicker and easier to bring me something else. Even if it's just swabs from the parents."

"Sure, one way or another, I'll get something to you. Thank you for your time Jane."

"Glad to help. I had a sister around Lette Walker's age when the news broke. I looked at her, and I thought about Lette, and that's when I decided to become a doctor."

"I'm sure her mother would love to know that; something good came from Lette's death. Or I suppose we should now be saying Lette's disappearance."

"Then tell her. Only maybe not the bit where I was too nervous about meeting patients in person and transferred across to dead people."

Phoebe grinned, "yes. Dead people don't try to second guess you, or argue back."

Jane smiled in acknowledgement, "would you let me know how you're getting on with this case? If it's not too much trouble I mean."

"Of course. I'll be coming back to you with the DNA soon, should we make an appointment to catch each other up?"

"Good idea," she said, grinning as she pulled out her phone, "my diary gets crazy busy if I don't get things in it first."

Jane suggested a time, and Lette wrote it down. "I have to get back to work now," she said, "but the meeting room is booked for another half an hour if you want to stay here to look through the file."

"Thanks, I will."

"Until Wednesday then," Jane said.

Phoebe stood to shake her hand once more, "I'm looking forward to it."

With Jane out of the room, she sat and read through the file.

As it turned out, Lette had disappeared, and someone else had been buried in her place.

So, what exactly had happened to Lette?

It seemed the next step ought to be checking in with the Walkers to find out what *really* happened the day Lette went missing.

«« • »»

The Walkers' house was a small, tired, dusty weatherboard on a quarter acre of dry grass.

Crowded out by new, or half-constructed modern triplexes and building sites.

Not a tree, or a bush, or a bird to be seen.

The sun's heat reflected off the road, brick and asbestos fences, and the concrete façades of the neighbouring properties.

Phoebe knocked on the door, which opened a crack. She looked at it.

"Hello?" she called, "hello Mrs Walker?"

Heavy footsteps rushed up the hall, and she took a step back, just in time to give free rein for a teenage boy to storm out of the house.

She turned to watch him go as he turned, scowling, to flip the bird back at the house.

She heard slippers scuffing up the hall and turned back to the house.

"Greg," Mrs Walker called, "Greg wait. Your father didn't mean—"

Her voice cut out as she caught sight of Phoebe.

Greg paused for a moment as she asked, "Phoebe, what are you doing here?"

Greg nodded, as if she'd answered a question, and walked away down the sidewalk, throwing his backpack on his back.

"Greg," Mrs Walker called, raising her hand towards him, clearly caught between running after him and getting rid of Phoebe.

She sighed, and turned towards Phoebe, "how can I help you Miss Swan?"

"Don't mind me, if you need to go after your son, I can wait."

"Not at all, come inside."

She followed the woman's back down a long hall and through to a large combined kitchen-dining room that didn't seem to have been updated since the seventies, with brown mosaic tiles on the benches and orange florals on the floor.

Mr John Walker was sitting at a round table that was too small for the space.

"Can I make you a cup of tea Phoebe?"

"Just let her spit out what she came for," he growled.

Phoebe didn't remember him being quite this aggressive during her Police enquiries. "Do you mind if I sit down?" she asked pointedly.

John, clearly still annoyed by his son's departure, kicked a chair out from under the table.

Phoebe decided in that moment not to mention that the dead girl wasn't Lette.

Or that there was any hint of anything odd about the autopsy.

But she had to be subtle about it.

"Lette's remains are with the Victorian Institute of Forensic Medicine, and they're about to redo the autopsy."

"Why the hell would they do that," John asked.

"Is that not what you had her exhumed for?"

He glared at his wife. There was definitely something going on between them, but Phoebe couldn't guess what it was.

She made a mental note to follow up on what exactly John Walker had been doing when Lette was kidnapped, and since then

After a pause, where no one said anything, Phoebe continued.

"Not to worry, the initial autopsy was cursory, and as the progress of forensic science has been remarkable in the last few years, there may be additional information that comes to light this time.

"Can you tell me anything further about the last day you saw Lette?"

"We told you all about that at the time."

"That isn't exactly how I would describe it, Mr Walker," she consulted her notes, "you said you had dropped her off at her fish and chip shop job about seven o'clock, and when you went back for her at 11, she had left to walk home. You followed the most likely route, but didn't see her."

"Sounds about right."

"Why would your sixteen-year-old daughter start walking home Mr Walker, "wouldn't she have waited for you?"

"I don't remember."

"I think you can Mr Walker, I think you can remember exactly what happened and choose not to tell me."

He stood up so abruptly his chair skittered across the floor, "I don't have to listen to this, I haven't done anything wrong," he said.

"Then why won't you tell me?"

He stalked out.

She turned to Mrs Walker, who had stopped just inside the room, wringing her hands.

"What about you Mrs Walker?"

"I don't know anything. I was at the supermarket stacking shelves from about five until about midnight. When I got home the house was dark and I assumed everyone was tucked up in bed."

"Are you telling me your husband had gone to bed when he knew your daughter was missing?"

"Well, they'd been fighting— I've said too much."

Phoebe made a mental note to follow up on her alibi as well.

"Fighting about what Mrs Walker?"

"Oh, you know the stuff. Hem to short, too makeup, going out with a hoodlum. John thought Lette was growing up too fast, and too wild."

That was the problem when you came to a case thinking it was one thing, and it turned out to be another one entirely.

"What about Greg?"

"Oh, he was only five years old at the time, change of life baby and all that. On a normal night, John would have stayed home to look after him, but I think he'd stayed over at a friend's house."

She'd already heard a lot that hadn't come out at the time.

Certainly a lot that needed to be corroborated.

"I think I have enough for now, but I'd hoped to get another DNA sample. If you don't have anything of Lette's anymore, I could a sample from both your husband and yourself."

John Walker came back into the kitchen at that point, "then you can take mine as long as you bugger off out of this house."

Phoebe took a swab from him, and his wife, and left the house.

Going back to her office via the VIFM for analysis.

«« • »»

Back in her grey cubicle at the Wilkinson's Collins Street office, she sorted through the file to see where she was up to.

The VIFM was looking at the body end of things.

She was about to investigate the family.

There was still the money to be found.

She was in two minds about whether to look into Mason, but there was no need to do it straight away. The most important thing was probably to look into the family first.

They married a couple of years before Lette was born, and bought the house that same year for $135,000. Taken out a second mortgage for the ransom, and the bank foreclosed shortly after.

They sold it for less than was owing.

John Walker had a relatively stable career, the last decade or so as a car salesman. No wonder he was highly irritable.

Prior to that...

He'd taken an apprenticeship in the Dahlia Funeral Home...

At the conclusion of his apprenticeship, he'd stayed on until they held his daughter's funeral.

And if the VIFM found the identity of the girl buried in Lette's place, Phoebe was prepared to wager the funeral had been one of the Dahlia Funeral Home's.

It was entirely possible that he'd had enough of the funeral industry after Lette died.

But it was equally possible that something had happened and they'd not only fired him, but blacklisted him throughout the industry.

She checked the business ownership; husband and wife team, transferring the business to their son. The names were familiar; the couple who owned the business, were the couple who'd bought the Walker's house.

They'd bought the house *after* he'd moved into car sales.

Were they good friends, or had there been some kind of blackmail or extortion incident? If she checked their banking records, would she find a deposit of $100,000; the money that was supposed to be paid to the kidnappers?

There was evidence of ongoing repayments to the bank, but no trace of rent payments, or perhaps repayments on an informal loan.

So, something to park, but not make any further enquiries until she could establish more information without approaching either couple.

Mrs Walker had an alibi; that she'd been working, so Phoebe's next step was to call the supermarket.

Happily, the woman who'd been her supervisor at the time was still working for the company, albeit in a different position.

Phoebe didn't hold out much hope of anything useful.

"Oh yes Miss Swan," she said, "I remember the night very well, because the thing about Lette was all over the news the next day. And Grace was definitely there that night.

"Except for her "lunch" break, she said she just had to run out for an errand. She was only supposed to be half an hour, but ended up taking a little over an hour."

So effectively Mrs Walker's alibi was shot.

She was clicking her fingernails on the surface of her desk, trying to work out what to look at next, when her phone rang.

Greg Walker was in the downstairs reception wanting to speak to her. She asked them to set up a small interview room for her and went down to see him.

He was around five years old when Lette went missing, so would he be able to offer anything concrete to her investigation?

Greg was a little nervous, looking around in case someone had followed him. She offered him a seat and he took it, but couldn't seem to settle.

She took the seat opposite him, "you asked to see me?"

"There's more to this than they're letting on," he said.

"Your parents?"

"Yes. They have strong religious beliefs, that's what we were arguing about. They want me to do something I don't want to do."

"Like stay home and study?"

"No, like go out and proselytise."

"Like the Witnesses or Scientologist?"

He made a sound of exasperation, "no. Like Charles Manson, or the People's Temple."

Phoebe sat up and regarded him steadily. He returned her gaze, with the right amount of eye contact. His breathing was even, and his voice steady. "You think they did something to Lette?"

"She was afraid of them. They didn't like that she was seeing an outsider—

"I mean I say outsider, but I mean someone outside the group. She'd been promised to a boy in the group a few years older than her when she was a child, and she was to be sent to him on her sixteenth birthday."

"Do you think that's where she is?" Phoebe asked.

"No. I think they killed her because she wanted to leave the church."

"That's a little extreme don't you think?"

He sighed and scrubbed his face with both hands. "They signed a contract, and there were penalties for not passing her over."

"But the legal age of marriage is 18."

"They'd gone to court, arguing exceptional and unusual circumstances, and a magistrate made the Order."

"What were the circumstances?"

"I don't know, I was only a child. Can't you look it up?"

"I can, I just wondered if you knew. When do you think they killed her?"

"The night she was," he held his fingers up, gesturing air quotes, "'kidnapped', they sent me to my friend's house to sleepover." He slumped in his chair, "I didn't have a clue what they were up to or I would have warned her.

"I should have warned her."

Phoebe did not reach out to pat his hand, "you did the best you could."

He pulled a tissue from his pocket and blew his nose.

"Now it's my turn. They've arranged a marriage for me, and I don't want any part of it. I've got a flight to Sydney this afternoon, and after that, I'm not saying what my plans are.

"But if I turn up dead, it's because of them."

"Is there anything I can do to help," Phoebe asked, but she bloody hoped not.

"Nah," he said with a faint smile, "you need to stay clear of this one. I can take care of myself."

He stood up, and picked up his backpack, "I'll be off now, I've done what I came to do. I hope wherever she is, Lette can forgive me."

Phoebe extended her hand, "then I wish you good luck. And if you ever need to find me, well, you know where I am."

«« • »»

Phoebe called Jane and arranged to meet her the next day.

"We now know the identity of our dead girl; Serena Hoskins."

"And was the funeral held by Dahlia Funeral Home?"

Jane consulted her notes, "how did you know?"

"John Walker, Lette's father worked there."

"Funny you should say that. I had Serena's remains sampled, and the DNA is a match to Grace Walker, but John Walker is not the father."

"That is insane!" Phoebe said.

"I know."

"The Walkers were apparently in a cult, and their son thinks they may have been responsible for Lette's murder."

"I can't believe that. In this day and age?"

"So, we've figured out who the bodies are, a possible motive, and probably where the money went. I think it's time to turn the evidence over to the Police."

《《 • 》》

Phoebe was at the Walker's house the day the Police came to arrest them.

"I knew you would work it out," Mrs Walker said as they handcuffed her, "the guilt has been eating me alive."

Phoebe didn't say anything, just closed the door behind her.

《《 • 》》

A few days later, a postcard featuring a picture of a large basket of roses arrived at the office.

"Good job," it said.

THE END

ABOUT THE AUTHOR

Alexandria Blaelock writes stories, some of them for *Ellery Queen's Mystery Magazine* and *Pulphouse Fiction Magazine.*

She's also written five selfhelp books applying business techniques to personal matters like getting dressed, cleaning house, and feeding your friends.

She lives in a forest because she enjoys birdsong, and the smell of gum leaves. When not telecommuting to parallel universes from her Melbourne based imagination, she watches K-dramas, talks to animals, and drinks Campari. At the same time.
Discover more at www.alexandriablaelock.com.

... or the first Georgia Garside

The Robin Hood of Private Investigators

Georgia Garside. Foul-mouthed Private
Investigator. Ex-contorionist.

Out of her depth. In over her head.

Caught up in the war between a wealthy
industrialist and the ex-sugar babe who can't take a
hint.

A laugh-out-loud tripartite battle of wits, winner
takes all.